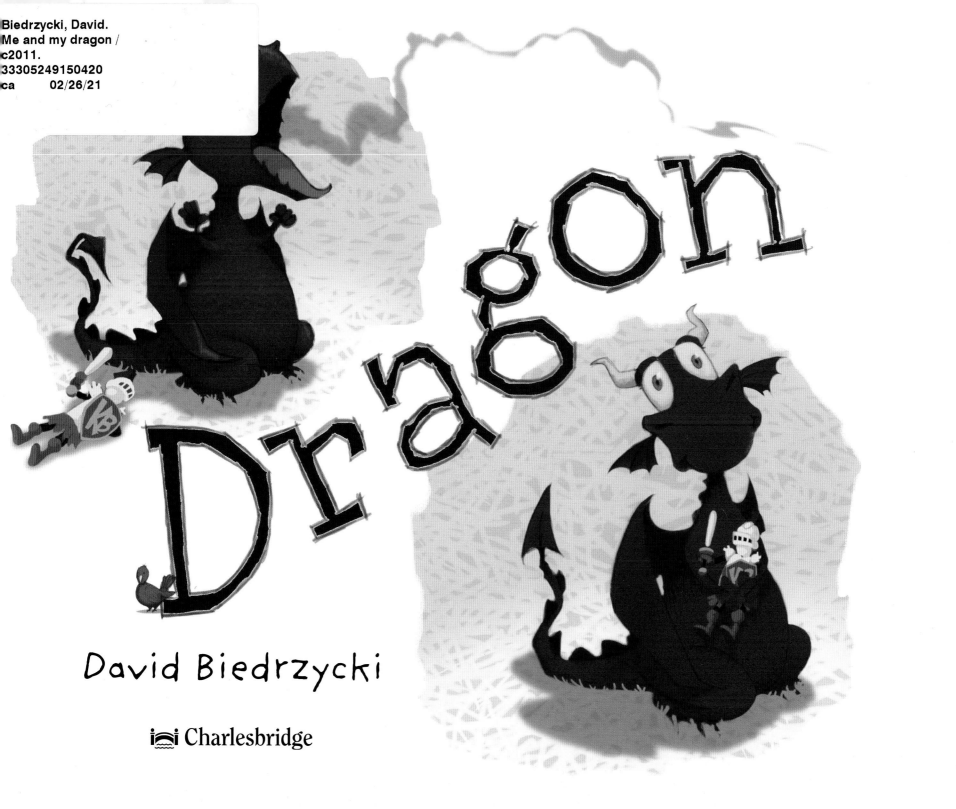

# Dragon

## David Biedrzycki

**ini Charlesbridge**

To my friends at the Ledyard Center School, where it all began
—D. B.

Published by Charlesbridge
85 Main Street
Watertown, MA 02472
(617) 926-0329
www.charlesbridge.com

Library of Congress Cataloging-in-Publication Data
Biedrzycki, David.
    Me and my dragon / David Biedrzycki.
      p. cm.
    Summary: A child tells all the reasons a small, fire-
breathing dragon would make an excellent pet, and the
ways to take proper care of it.
      ISBN 978-1-58089-278-0 (reinforced for library use)
      ISBN 978-1-58089-279-7 (softcover)
      ISBN 978-1-60734-309-7 (ebook pdf)
[1. Dragons—Fiction. 2. Pets—Fiction.] I. Title.
PZ7.B4745Me 2011
[E]—dc22              2010023527

Printed in China
(hc) 10 9 8 7
(sc) 10

Illustrations done in Adobe Photoshop
Display type and text type set in Jellygest
    and Providence Sans
Color separations by Chroma Graphics, Singapore
Printed by Imago in China
Production supervision by Brian G. Walker
Designed by Diane M. Earley

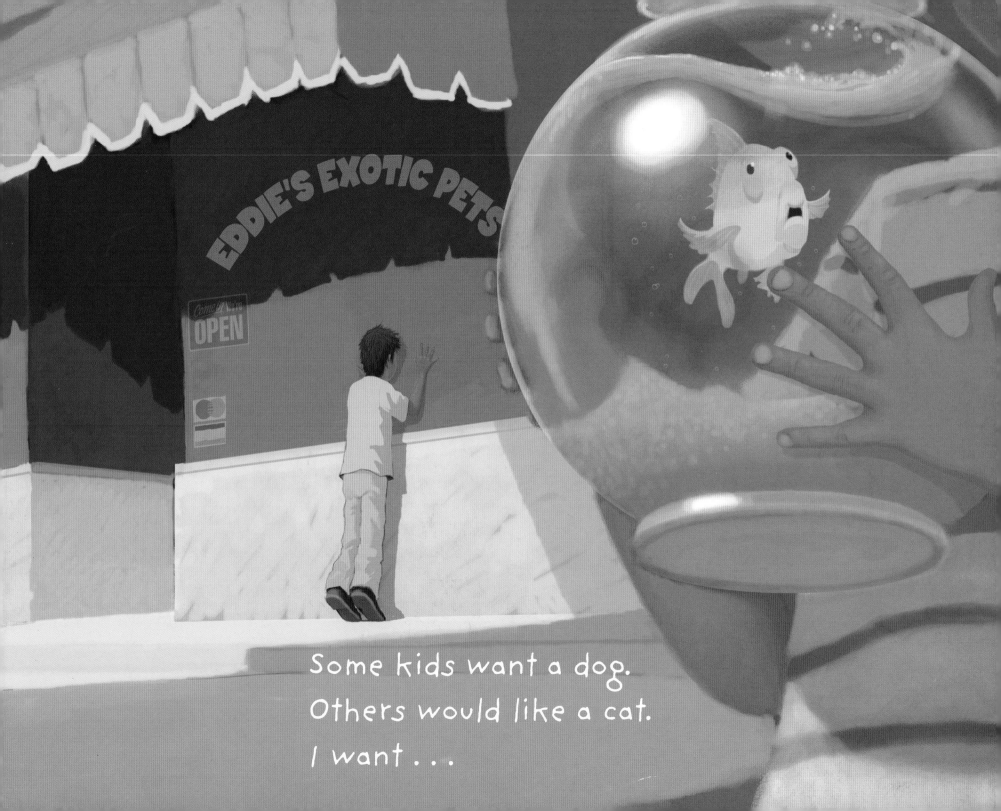

Some kids want a dog.
Others would like a cat.
I want . . .

But not a big dragon.
A big dragon wouldn't
fit in my house.

I wouldn't want a
three-headed dragon either.
It might not get along
with itself.

I'd choose a fire-breathing dragon.

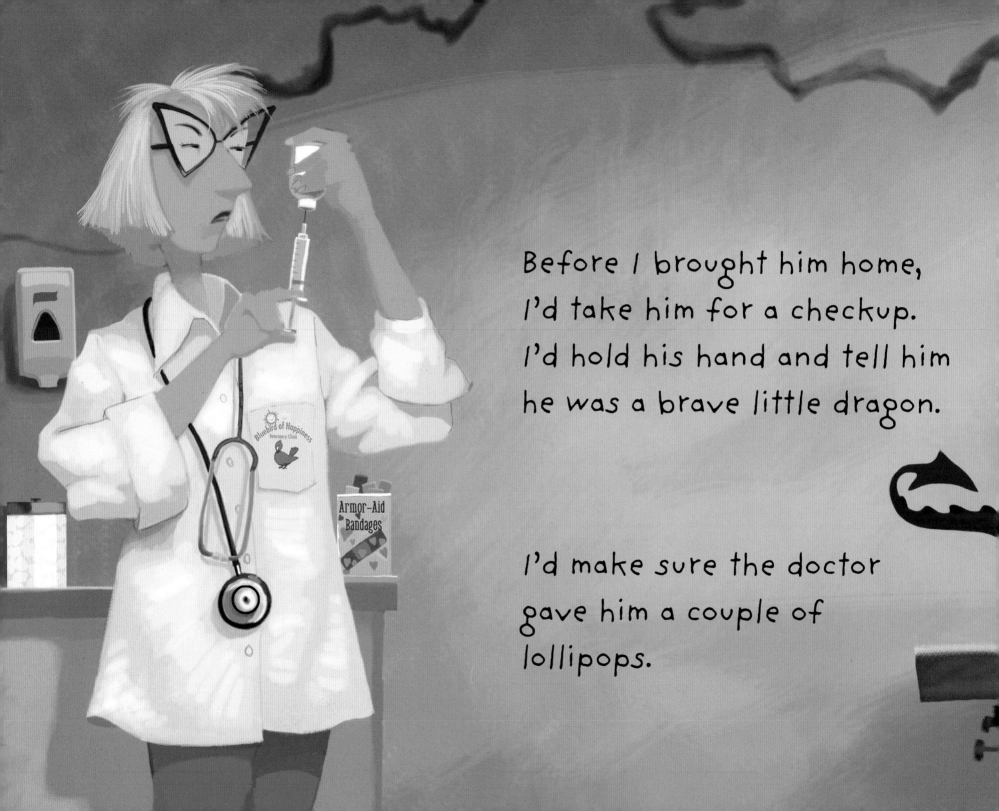

Before I brought him home,
I'd take him for a checkup.
I'd hold his hand and tell him
he was a brave little dragon.

I'd make sure the doctor
gave him a couple of
lollipops.

On the way home
he could sit with me,
if Mom and Dad
didn't mind.

I'd give him a name, a place to stay, and some toys to play with.

When I thought he was ready,
I'd teach him to fly.

I'd get him a collar and a leash.
Then I'd take him for
a walk every day.

If he was a naughty dragon . . .

After he learned to behave,
I could take him camping
in the summer

and trick-or-treating
in the fall.

Nice costume!

We could clear neighbors'
driveways in the winter.

But I might not take him kite flying in the spring.

If I missed the bus, he would help me get to school just in time for show-and-tell.

Bullies?

You don't need to worry about
brussels sprouts either.
Dragons love 'em.

(But don't give them broccoli.
It gives them gas. And you
don't want a fire-breathing
dragon with gas.)

Every night I'd give my dragon a bath. Bath time would be fun.

Sometimes.

I would pick out books that wouldn't give him nightmares and read to him until he got sleepy.

I'd tuck him in and say good night.
Then we'd fall asleep.
Just me and my dragon.